Orville Right-Fly Boy

Douglas Van Wyk

Illustrated by Gail Nelson

To Julie! Enjoy!

ISBN 1-4196-2801-1

To order additional copies, please contact us.
BookSurge, LLC
www.booksurge.com
1-866-308-6235
orders@booksurge.com

To Lisa, Jonathan, Rachel, James R., and my sixth graders at TKA

1

Orville woke up from his sound sleep once again. He had been dreaming again — the same dream he had every night. From his earliest childhood, he had dreams of flying. In his dreams, he would flap his arms gently, and his body would rise and hover above the quaint little streets of Monterey where he and his Aunt Hilda lived. When Orville was only two, his mother and father had died in a car accident. Hilda Klompmacher, his mother's sister, told the rest of the family that she would be little Orville's guardian. Though she played the role of a good sister, she resented him for all the hours it took to feed and care for him, and she secretly wanted out of the responsibility. But she begrudgingly stuck with him anyway. She was a waitress at Denny's, and she was hardly ever home to take care of Orville. He had pretty much learned to take care of himself.

As Orville grew up, he was very lonely. He had seen superheroes on television as he wiled away the hours at home and his Aunt Hilda worked at Denny's. At night, when he went to sleep, he kept having the same dream about flying, and this was his favorite dream of all. These dreams were so exciting that he would actually wake up afterward with the intense desire to fly and hover above the clouds. Only he knew this was silly. But if he could fly like a superhero, he would try to give something back to the world.

One day, as he was preparing his breakfast of Lucky Charms and orange juice, Orville decided to try something different and mix some of his chewable vitamins into the Lucky Charms. He thought they would make a good combination because they looked so similar to each other. Both were colorful and shaped like animals, moons, hearts, and four-leaf clovers. As he ate his new concoction, little did he know about the permanent physical changes going on inside his tiny body. He started to feel very funny and warm all over. He stepped into the back yard. A picture began developing in his mind as he stood there on the patio. He was rising slowly in the air in this picture, and he was only moving his arms slightly. He felt as light as a butterfly, but he could not explain why.

Suddenly, little Orville realized that he was not dreaming! He actually was hovering over his own backyard, about twenty feet up in the air! He could see his own feet below him just hanging there, useless. He felt marvelous and ecstatic, as he hung there in the atmosphere, and it was the best feeling he ever had. The wind was blowing in his face gently, the sun was shining, and life was suddenly amazing and wonderful for little Orville Klompmacher.

Orville experimented with his newfound flying ability. He leaned to the left and went left. He veered to the right and soared up to a branch in the oak tree by the shed, but got a bit scratched up from hitting some of the tree limbs. For the next hour, he was tipsy and unsure of himself, and when he landed on the cat at about 5 PM, the neighbors ran over to see if everything was okay. As day began to turn into night, he tested himself repeatedly and found that by sheer will power, he could actually fly! As his aunt pulled in the driveway again at 8 PM that evening, he was hiding under the covers of his bed. He giggled to himself, thinking about how he was now an experienced flier, and she didn't even know about it.

The next day, as he was getting ready for bed, Orville felt the urge to fly come over him once again. It made him tingle all over, and he again felt lighter than air. He moved his arms, and he started to float out of the window, like Peter Pan. He rose into the night sky, higher and higher, and he felt as if he could stay there forever. As the stars twinkled in the night sky over Monterey, Orville felt updrafts carry him higher and higher. He was pushing the envelope tonight!

He swooped down and rose up higher still, as the air grew colder and colder. He felt as if he was struggling to breathe as he rose, so he started to flap his arms less and let himself slowly descend.

Into his bedroom window he went. The joy and exhiliration he felt was amazing. Orville thought to himself that night about what to tell his Aunt Hilda. He knew she didn't like him very much. The way she spoke to him was rough, and she never hugged him, smiled at him, or said that she loved him. So he decided to keep his secret to himself as long as he could. Every night, he would go out flying when everyone else was asleep, and for years this went on. He saw the ocean, enjoyed the beautiful mountains, and soared through the valleys of the California coast. All was right with the world when Orville was flying in those wee hours of the morning. Sometimes he would land and just enjoy nature. He'd sit on the rocks and watch the surf come in and out. Or he would fly to the top of a redwood tree and just sit there for hours, listening to the birds and watching the seagulls fly through the evening sky by the hundreds. Once, as he was flying over the Pacific ocean on a moonlit evening, he even saw several whales lift their tails high in the air and slap them down on the peaceful swells.

As time went by, Orville could keep his miracle a secret no longer. During breakfast with his Aunt Hilda, he would tell her about his dreams and about his nightly adventures. She never believed his stories at all, and never even checked on him during the night to see if they were true. She didn't care one little bit about Orville. But the more he told her, the more she decided to investigate the matter. She arranged an appointment with a psychologist named Dr. William Landbound, and she told little Orville that she would take him there to help him get these crazy ideas about flying out of his head once and for all. They drove to downtown Monterey on a Monday morning in February. Orville didn't like the whole idea of this visit, but he slowly walked through the glass office doors, sat down, and read a magazine in the waiting room for what seemed like an eternity.

2

Finally, Dr. Landbound came to the door of the therapy room. "Come in, come in, Mr. Klompmacher! You've been waiting long enough. It's time we get down to business. I've heard all about your uh...issue."

"What issue?" asked Orville. "You're just like all the rest! No one believes me!"

"What others say does not matter! Of course you can fly, Orville! Your Aunt Hilda told me all about it. Or is it just a dream? A wonderful little game you are playing in your mind? Maybe we can get to the bottom of that! Let's see if I have some ink blots here... they're here somewhere. Ah yes, here we go! What do you see in this one?" asked the good doctor.

"Looks like clouds to me, "confessed Orville. "I've seen plenty of those! Gets cold up there!"

"Uh huh, yessssss," said Doctor Landbound.

"And this one?"

"Well, I hate to say it, but to me it looks like um, like... birds flying through clouds," admitted Orville.

"Perhaps now would be a good time for me to get my gold watch," sighed Dr. Landbound. The doctor began swinging the watch back and forth. "You are getting sleepy, Orville. Very sleepy. Just relax and tell me all about the flying."

"Well, it's nothing really," replied Orville dreamily.

"I just wave my arms up and down really fast, and I start going up. It's wonderful! Once I get up high, I keep waving and I can go anywhere - at least most of the time. Sometimes I start sinking. Other times I speed up or slow down without trying- I haven't quite got it under control."

"Repeat after me... My arms are not wings. I am not a bird."

"I am not a bird." repeated Orville.

"That's right," chanted the doctor.

"But I can fly. When I fly, I don't want to come down, but I do it anyway so that no one worries where I went."

Right about then, something weird happened. Orville's arms started flapping and he took off from the couch of Doctor Landbound's office. His arms were gently flapping, even while he was under hypnosis.

The doctor could not believe his eyes. As he gazed in wonder at the flying Orville, he noticed that Orville was waking up.

"I told you I could fly!" shouted Orville. "See you later, Doc!" he screamed as he flew out the window. Over the city streets Orville hovered and flapped. He felt like he could fly forever, and his arms were working effortlessly. As he floated dreamily over the streets of Monterey, he noticed a little old lady wearing a flower-covered dress. A one-armed man, dressed in black, had just grabbed her purse and was running away.

"Stop, You crook!" shouted Orville. He flew down toward the bandit, forgetting all his fears and inhibitions. It was like he was someone else - a crime fighter - a righter of wrongs - a do-gooder!

"I don't like the name Orville Klompmacher!" thought Orville. "From now on, I want to be Orville Right, Fly-Boy - righter of wrongs and rescuer of the less-than-fortunate! Yeah, that sounds pretty good!"

Orville zoomed in low and almost hit the ground when he lost power for a moment. Then he hooked the purse right out of the bandit's hand with his foot. POW! He kicked him in the head! Orville then flew several blocks and found the old woman who had been victimized.

"Fear no more, ma'am!" said Orville. "Your purse is safe and so are you! I'll report this to the authorities immediately!"

And so he did. He landed right in front of the 31st street police station. Officer Bookem took his statement, and within minutes, an all-points-bulletin was sent out to capture the bandit. Orville quickly sneaked out of the building after making the report. The officer never did find out his real name, since he made up a fictitious name. Headlines in the next day's newspaper reported the incident - "Flying Boy Rescues Elderly Woman."

Yes, it was a big day for Orville Right. As he walked home, he reveled in his accomplishment secretly because the newspaper never said his real name. The old lady didn't know it either, but Orville knew the truth. He was on his way to a life of service to those in need. He would use his amazing gift to help his fellow man - even if his Aunt Hilda didn't believe he could fly! He crept into the house quietly, without his aunt even knowing it, and went to sleep on his Captain America bed.

3

After that amazing Monday, Tuesday rolled around. Orville was so excited as he read the morning paper that he could hardly stand it.

"To think, this is ME they're talking about in the newspaper! I'm a hero!"

"Orville, it's time to take out the trash!" shouted Aunt Hilda. Orville could not help but think that such a thing was beneath him, with him being a hero and all.

"But I've got something important to tell you!" he answered. "You're not going to believe it, Aunt Hilda! You know how you sent me to the doctor, because you didn't think I could fly? Well, it's time I showed you once and for all!"

"Don't talk nonsense, boy!" screamed his aunt. "Arms don't work for flying, and you know it. Wait 'til I get my hands on that doctor. It sounds like your seeing him didn't help much!"

"But watch, Auntie! I'll show you once and for all!" And at that moment, Orville flapped his arms and rose into the air, above the bed in his room! There was no reasonable or logical explanation for it. It was beyond explanation. This was mysterious and unexplainable stuff, and both of them knew it.

"AHHHHHHH!" shrieked Aunt Hilda. She had heard him talking about this flying stuff before, but she had always thought he was just making it all up. "How'd you do that? That's not possible! I'm losing my mind!"

"That's the cool part, Aunt Hilda! It's a miracle! But it's amazing, huh? Just yesterday, I was flying over the city and I rescued this little old lady from a purse snatcher! It was so cool, I couldn't believe it!" exclaimed Orville.

"Well, you just calm down there, son. Just let yourself back down on the bed for a minute!" she said. Orville stopped flapping and descended to the bed. "You've had a big day, all right. Why don't you just get some rest and relax for a while? I'll make you a nice, hot Sloppy Joe for lunch, and I'll call you when it's ready."

"Sounds good to me!" yawned Orville. He was quite sleepy after Monday, and he quickly drifted off. Meanwhile, Aunt Hilda had a trick up her sleeve.

"Hello, Dr. Landbound? Have I got something to tell you!" she yelled into the phone.

"And I've got something to tell you!" he replied. "He really CAN fly! He flew right out my office window! Did you read today's paper? It's unbelievable!

"Of course I did, you twit! I found out myself just minutes ago!" she retorted.

"We've got to find out what makes him tick... what gives him this marvelous ability!" stated Dr. Landbound. "Why don't you bring him to the hospital, and we can examine him?

"Okay, I'll try. I know! I can lie to him and say we're going somewhere else. Then he won't know anything about our little plan here... and maybe I can slip something in his food to make him drowsy," she said schemingly.

"Alright, bring him here at 2 p.m. this afternoon."

"Yes, I'll be there. We might be able to make a fortune from this! No more waitressing at Denny's anymore!" said Aunt Hilda.

4

So 1:30 PM arrived. Orville was full after his delicious sandwich, and he was anxious to go the mall. He wanted to check out their costume department for a superhero outfit. He wouldn't do it when Hilda was looking, he decided. Somehow, he'd just gather the information and shop without buying today.

"This doesn't seem like the way we usually go, Aunt Hilda." said Orville. "Where are we going?"

"I have to stop at the drug store next to the hospital, first," she lied.

"Okay, whatever..." said Orville. "But can we hurry?"

"Sure thing, Orville."

Suddenly Orville felt very groggy. He could hardly see straight. The next thing he knew, he was on an examining table in the hospital, and he was strapped down tightly. He could barely move! Dr. Landbound, Hilda, and two other nurses were standing over him, looking at him like he was some kind of specimen under a microscope.

Obviously, Orville was pretty frightened by all this attention. He wasn't sure what to do first. Should he try to fly away again? Or was it no use? His hands and legs were tied down tightly. He felt like a trapped animal, and he couldn't believe his own aunt could do such a thing to him. He looked around the room and gazed in wild wonder at the huge tubes, the metal surfaces, and the incredibly large, expensive machines.

"Orville, I know you think the worst of us right now," said Doctor Landbound. "But we've just got to figure out what makes you tick!"

"You mean what makes me fly!" said Orville.

"Exactly!" retorted the doctor. "And when we do, you will make medical history! Why, there's no end to the mon... I mean the attention that we... I mean, you, will get from all this. You'll go down in history as the boy who could fly! Superman, move over!"

"I don't want anyone to know who I really am," said Orville. He didn't want all the attention. He didn't want people to think he was weird or to want his autograph or anything else like that. He just wanted to help people if he could - using his gift - and he wanted to keep his saving work a secret, just like Superman. Yes, he knew he was no Superman, but he thought he could do some good anyway.

"Why don't you just let me do what I want?" Orville asked. "You can still study me if you want, but don't hold me prisoner! I need to get out of here. This is no place for a person like me to be. I should be in the air flying free and soaring over rivers and mountains and lakes. I just love being up there and feeling like I can float over the world! I probably can't save many people anyway!"

"There will be time for that all, Orville!" said Aunt Hilda. "We'll let you go soon enough. We just don't want you flying away! Who knows when we will see you again? You might be gone for days, and I'd be worried sick about you. You know you're the only family I've got. All we've got is each other!"

"Okay, just untie me, and I promise I won't try to fly away," pleaded Orville.

So they untied him. But once they released his bonds

he realized that he had a very long rope attached to his leg, and it was shackled to him, so that he couldn't get it off without a key.

"What in the world is this?" asked the young fly-boy.

"It's a tether," said the doctor. "We need you to come outside with us and show us a few of your flying tricks. Maybe somehow we can figure out what's going on in that body of yours."

"But you're never going to find that out!" cried Orville. "It's not something you can explain away with science! It's magic or supernatural or something like that!"

Well, that didn't satisfy the doctor or his own Aunt Hilda. Being the scientific type, Landbound had to analyze and study him. As they came to the top floor of the hospital, Orville noticed that there was a helicopter pad there. They were going on the roof of the building to get him to fly on a leash!

"Okay, Orville. We're here now. Are you ready? Flap your arms and let's see you do this," commanded Doctor Landbound.

So Orville flapped. He flapped until his body began to rise and he was hovering over the heliopad. The tether held him in one place, and it made flying almost impossible. There was no joy in this. No freedom, no soaring, no wonderful rush. He felt like a captive bird.

The doctor was writing furiously, taking notes on everything he observed, as a good scientist does. Aunt Hilda was snapping pictures like there was no tomorrow, and talking incessantly on her cell phone. He guessed that she was calling the newspaper or something ridiculous and dumb like that. He didn't trust her at all anymore, and he felt betrayed by her, as anyone would.

"Can I come down now?" asked the weary little bird.

"Stay up as long as you can, Orville! We need to know how long you can do this. You've been up for about five minutes now. Are you tired? Describe to me what you are feeling or experiencing. I want to know it all. Fly, my boy, fly!" shouted the doctor.

"I feel like I am floating, like my body is lighter than air." said Orville. "I feel as if my arms could fly forever and never get tired. Even if I knew how I can fly, I'd never tell you! You'll never figure it out through science either!" he shouted from above.

Suddenly, a strange thing happened. All over the rooftop, there were reporters, TV cameramen, sound crews, and lighting crews. Orville had become the evening news once again, only this time his identity was going to be public. Pictures were being taken rapid-fire. Flashes from the cameras filled the sky and everywhere he looked, Orville saw people. There was not even room for him to land, there were so many TV people everywhere.

And who was this coming toward him? None other than Ed Murray, the news anchorman! "Ladies and gentlemen! We are gathered on this rooftop to see a truly amazing miracle! Orville Right, who lives with his Aunt Hilda in Monterey California, is flying over our heads as we speak, and he is flying under his own power!" screamed Ed. "This is astounding! It's like nothing I've ever seen! This is no comic book fiction hero, ladies and gentlemen, and it's not a movie either. This is a supernatural act you are seeing live on this channel!"

By now, Orville was tired. He was not physically tired, however. He was tired of flapping and flapping and not getting anywhere. He was tired of people treating him like he was King Kong or something. The similarities between him and Kong were quite amazing to say the least. Both were considered freaks by the media and subjected to all their abusive and selfish behaviors.

"I'M NOT GOING TO DO THIS ANYMORE!" he shouted from the top of his lungs. Orville then stopped flapping his arms. He slowly descended to the rooftop. Reporters and television people pounced on him and grabbed him. They pushed him and questioned him and shoved microphones in his face.

"What's it like Orville? To fly? How do you do it? When did you first find out you could fly? How fast can you go? Do you get tired? How far can you fly?" The questions never stopped, and Orville had bruises all over him from the people stepping on him, tearing at his clothes, and trying to get at him. Orville wished he had never been born.

5

Orville was finally rescued from the crowd by his Aunt Hilda, the same Aunt Hilda who had made all the necessary phone calls to get him on the air that night – and I don't mean flying in the air. He sat in his hospital room, watching the little suspended television in the far corner of the room. He was one unhappy fly-boy, even though he was on the evening news. This was not the kind of publicity he wanted. No rescuing done that day. No soaring or catching updrafts for him either. No warm summer breeze in his face. What was the point of having this wonderful gift, when all the people around him just wanted to muck things up?

"I can't believe that the whole world knows this!" Orville said to himself. "They know my name, they know I can fly, and they know where I live. I'll never be able to go anywhere or be unnoticed again. This is terrible! And just when I thought maybe I could make a difference in the world – like maybe helping someone like that little old lady again."

As Orville looked around the room, he noticed that his eyelids were very heavy. He had been drugged! There was no way he was going to fly out the window here! Not only was he drugged – there was no window!

When he finally did awake, Orville found himself in the back of a van. He was blindfolded, and his hands were tied with duct tape, like a ransom victim or something. He couldn't believe this was happening to him, and he couldn't believe that his own aunt would do such a treacherous thing to him. He kept working his hands back and forth, and he finally managed to wiggle out of the duct tape. He ripped the blindfold off, and decided that the minute the doors opened, he would do everything in his power to make a run for it and fly away.

He could feel that the van was making a number of turns, left and right, but he didn't try to count them. He had no idea how long they had been driving before he woke up, so it seemed pointless to try to determine his location that way. He heard muffled sounds outside, but again, they were no help at all. He could also hear voices in the van. Muffled as they were, it was impossible to understand them. Suddenly, the van stopped. The rear doors flew open.

"Come on, Orville!" said Aunt Hilda. "It's time to find a safer place for you to be, where the crowds can't bother you."

Orville didn't wait for them to grab him and drag him off. He leaped from the back of the van and shot into the sky like a rocket. He had a newfound strength and an incredible amount of energy at this point in time, and as he soared over the ocean, he knew it was because he had had a good rest and was determined to escape. He didn't care about Aunt Hilda anymore. He would fend for himself, find his own food, and make his own shelter. He came to the conclusion that living in a cardboard box would be better than living with her, even if she was a blood relative.

As Orville pondered these things, he had been soaring along the coast. There were beautiful trees everywhere. He decided that he was still somewhere along the coast of Monterey, where the most beautiful scenery in the world is. The sun was shining brightly, which doesn't happen very often along the

California coast. Seagulls were gathering by the hundreds for a group attack against a school of fish below. Orville could see tourists watching him and clicking the shutters of their digital cameras. They were taking more pictures of him than of their own families! Orville felt a tremendous rush from all that he'd accomplished. He had escaped, at last! No more tethers and no more observations. No more quack psychologists treating him like an ape under study!

The updrafts were amazing today. Orville hardly had to flap his arms at all. He just held them at his sides and climbed higher and higher toward the sun. As he did so, he couldn't help but think of the story of Icarus, who invented wings out of wax and feathers. The mistake Icarus made was that he flew so close to the sun that the wax melted, and he fell to his death. No such troubles for Orville. There was no wax to melt. He just had to remember not to look at the sun too much. There was a part of him that wanted to keep soaring towards it – it felt so warm and inviting. But he knew that he had to focus. Flying too high would deprive him of oxygen. The air was getting colder, too, so he began to point his body downward and come in for a landing.

He searched the area near the coast for a good spot to land. Gently, he came down to a sidewalk near a 7 Eleven. No one had seen him land, as far as he could tell. He stopped in for a Slurpy. He knew he had a twenty dollar bill in his wallet, from some money he made mowing lawns. He was sure glad he had hung onto it – it was just such an emergency.

6

As he slurped, he walked toward a lovely bench that was placed in an immense and beautiful green lawn area. Cedar trees framed the lawn, and flowers by the thousands were fragrantly and visibly blessing the tourists. Suddenly, there was a scream from a thousands yards away. Even though it was a scream, it was barely audible to Orville because of the distance it was away. As he tried to determine where it was, he realized the sound was coming from an immense lighthouse next to the park.

"I've got to get over there fast!" Orville said to himself. He flew with all his might toward the spectacular lighthouse as its bright light slowly turned back and forth. There on the very top of the lighthouse, was a blonde-haired boy about the same age as Orville, standing on the catwalk with his body leaning over the railing. He was crying profusely and his legs were dangling further and further off the edge.

"How did you get up here?" cried Orville.

"I climbed up the stairs inside, like everybody else" returned the boy, shaking as he sobbed. "Just go away. I don't need you or anyone else! "

"Don't jump!" shouted Orville. "Whatever the reason for your jumping is, it isn't worth it!"

"I've got nobody who cares about me. My dad ran off and my mother's gone too. There's no more food in my house...

and I... I don't know what to do. Just let me get this over with."
The boy continued to dangle further and further over the ledge.

Orville knew he had to do something fast, or the boy would do what he said he'd do. He reached for the boy's arm to grab him, but over he went! Suddenly, the end was near! Orville leaped off the ledge and flew down to catch the boy just in time. Slowly, they descended to a stony driveway near the lighthouse.

"How did you do that?" asked the boy.

"Please, just come with me," said Orville. "We'll figure this out. I know what it's like to have no one who really cares for you. Maybe we can be friends and help each other figure out what to do next. What's your name, anyway?"

"Wilbur," said the young boy. "Hey, maybe we can build our own house in the woods near here. I know a really good place for it. At least if it rains tonight, we won't get soaked."

So Orville Right and his new friend Wilbur decided to help each other out. They found some large uneven sheets of discarded plywood near a home that was under construction and dragged them into the woods. They quickly placed them in a tree and created their own little Swiss Family Robinson tree house, full of amazing ropes, pulleys, nooks, and crannies. By day, they made money doing yardwork and walking people's dogs. The two of them were able to buy enough food to be quite happy, and there was no end to the kind deeds that they performed together.

For now, the fly-boy and his newfound friend were very happy. They didn't know what the future held, but things looked bright ahead. Maybe the two of them could invent something wonderful - something that would allow Wilbur to fly next to Orville and feel the same exhilaration that he felt. After all, they were both pretty handy. They had made an amazing tree house! Who knew what else they could accomplish together?

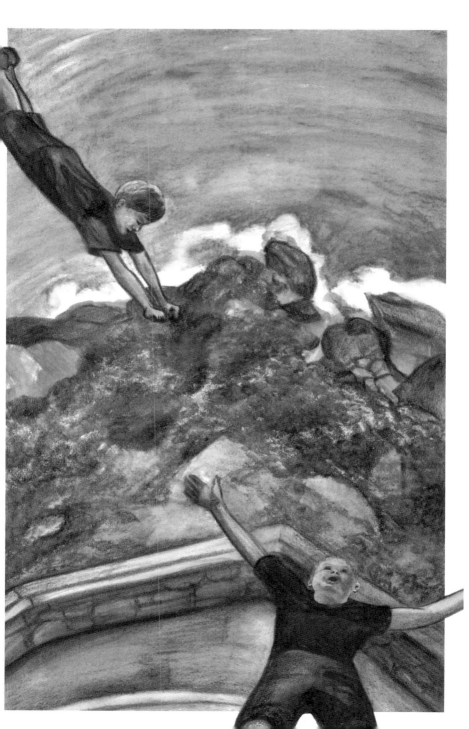

7

It didn't take long for Orville to realize that Wilbur was no ordinary boy. Before he knew it, Wilbur was scrounging around the neighborhood on a daily basis, looking for more scraps of lumber to create things wonderful.

"Hey Orville, did you see what I made?" shouted Wilbur as he scurried up into the tree house. "It's amazing and fantastic! I think it will really work! I tested it just a few minutes ago, and I must have flown for a few hundred feet!"

"You're kidding me! You didn't really fly! Where did you test it?" asked Orville.

"No, I'm not lying! It really worked! I tried it out by the water on the beach. The wind picked me up and I was soaring over the water, just like you! Come and look at it!" exclaimed Wilbur.

The two boys made their way down the trunk of the treehouse and headed for the beach. There, lying on a secluded area next to some enormous boulders, was the most beautiful hang-glider you ever laid eyes on. It was constructed with great care, and every hinge worked like a Swiss watch as Wilbur demonstrated.

"Let's try it out right now! You can fly next to me!" stammered the ecstatic Orville.

So as Orville flapped his arms and rose into the sky, the

gentle Monterey breeze picked little Wilbur and his hang-glider up like a mother cuddling her infant child. There was no end to the thrills the boys discovered as they flew along the coast of Highway 1 toward Santa Cruz. Cars below them were weaving in and out of the coastline, and ear-ringed bikers on their Harley-Davidsons couldn't help but look up when they noticed what looked like a hang-glider with two boys attached to it. Every now and then, Wilbur and Orville flew so close together that they appeared to be two passengers on the glider. What lay in store for them next would turn out to be a big surprise.

8

While Orville and Wilbur were having the time of their lives, there was another group of friends nearby living what they also considered the good life. These three men were a bit odd to say the least. They had met one another during the 1960s, when the Viet Nam war was in full swing. While serving in Nam together, they vowed that if they were single afterwards, they would look for one another again and maybe live the bachelor life in peace, with time for hunting, fishing, and similar adventures. After marriages, divorces, and various unhappy occurances, the three ended up living in a cabin in the hills of Santa Cruz, far from most of the other retirees their age.

Simon, the oldest of the three, suffered from too much exposure to Agent Orange. He saw things that weren't there, and he often had bad hallucinations that caused him to be downright scary to the people next door. They'd watch him over the fence and notice him staring up at the sky, grasping for what in his mind appeared to be giant flies. But of course, they didn't really exist. Overall, though, Simon was a good man. He loved to hunt in the hills, high up where there were no inhabitants except squirrels and jackrabbits. He also enjoyed hunting birds, when he happened to get lucky enough to spot them.

Now, the second veteran, named Sam, saw combat as well. After meeting Simon in boot camp, he moved on to becoming a jet mechanic, and Simon never heard what happened to him after that until later. The two found each other during their retirement years by writing letters and sending e-mails. Though the war had been hard on Sam too, he still had his wits about him, and he was the glue that held Simon together. Without Sam, Simon probably would have wandered into the hills and never returned.

Phil, on the other hand, was not a common soldier. He had worked as a navy seal after separating from Sam and Simon, and he had never told anyone about his clandestine operations. As the old saying goes, he could tell you about it, but then he'd have to kill you. But let it suffice to say that Navy Seals are a different breed. They never believe anything without proof of it, and they are skeptical about everything. But they are men of action, willing to take risks.

Well, our three retired war heroes were having a typical Wednesday afternoon when something very strange happened. It was pretty shocking to Simon, Sam, and Phil, because they were creatures of habit. You see, they had schedules that they stuck to, and Wednesday was always hunting day. Being retired, they had lots of time on their hands, and they knew just what to do with it on a daily basis.

"I sure hope we can find us some duck today," said Simon. "I'm almost sure I saw some flying in a huge flock right across this valley here yesterday."

"Yeah, sure, Si," returned Phil. "Kind of like you saw those 3-foot jackrabbits last week."

"Don't tell me what I saw or didn't see, you old coot!" said Simon, as he fumbled with his twelve-gauge shotgun. "I'm not as crazy as you two think I am! I know what I saw! Whoa! What was that?" said Simon. "It was one huge duck! I've never seen one that gigantic!"

"You crazy old loon!" called Sam. "Will you get a grip on

it? There are no monster ducks flying here or anywhere else!"
Phil put his safety on and tried to reach for Simon's gun before he
did something crazy.

"There it is! That baby's all mine! Oh yeah! We're gonna
have us some major duck helpings tonight!" screamed Simon.

Simon aimed high and shot before Sam had a chance to
stop him.

"That's no duck, you old fool! What did you do? That
looked more like a boy than a duck! I think there were two of
them! Oh no, they are boys!" shouted Phil as he watched them
fall from the sky.

The three men suddenly turned white with fear for what
Simon had done. Then they stopped to think about why a boy
was up in the sky in the first place.

"Did he have a hang-glider or something? Or a parachute?
What was that thing falling out of the sky next to them?" asked
Sam.

The threesome ran as quickly as they could to where they
suspected the boys had fallen. Sure enough, far down the trail
they could see two boys lying on the ground, near a small stream
that went past the men's cabin. Next to them there was a broken
hang-glider, fractured and splintered beyond recognition. In the
middle of the debris lay our heroes, Orville Right — Fly Boy
and his friend Wilbur. Orville had been flying under his own
miraculous power of course, and Wilbur had been enjoying some
great updrafts in his own homemade glider. It had been a great
afternoon like many others, until a crazy old man shot Orville
in the arm, and I think you know who that was. Wilbur had lost
control of his aircraft when trying to save Orville from falling to
his death. The two boys fell from the sky like baby birds out of
their mother's nest, but they landed safely as they were not that

high up. They tumbled through the branches of a few trees and this broke their fall somewhat. Finally they hit the ground and came to rest.

"My arm, my arm!" moaned Orville. "It hurts so bad! Help me Wilbur!"

"I think you're going to be okay, Orville," replied Wilbur. "It looks like they just winged you. No pun intended. See? It's just a scratch! And here you had to go falling out of the sky! Now look at us!"

"Who are those old men over there?" asked Orville. "Oh no! There coming after us! Run, Wilbur, run! This can't be a good thing! They'll probably turn us in or something! They could be rangers or worse yet — someone looking for us!"

The boys scurried off down the trail as fast as they could, but they were no match for our fearsome threesome — macho military men as they were.

"Whoa! Hold on there boys!" exclaimed Sam. "We're not the enemy! We're friends, don't worry! We just want to help!"

"Yeah, right!" said Wilbur. "Help us by shooting at us! What is it with you guys? Are you out of your minds?"

"Well, I guess you could say that," said Simon, matter of factly.

"Speak for yourself, Simon!" said Phil.

"Will you two just shut your yaps long enough for us to figure this out?" reprimanded Sam. "Now just what were you two doing up there? How is it that only one of you was in the hang-glider? That doesn't make a whole lot of sense."

"Well," said Orville. "Uh, yeah. Right. Um, well... I guess you could say I was flying on my own. Uh-huh. That's it."

"Okay, that clears up everything! Now I completely understand!" said Phil. "And I suppose your Superboy? Nice to meet you, Boy Wonder! I'm Batman! Just kidding — Phil's the name."

"I think he was hanging on to the glider or something," said Sam.

"No, he wasn't, Sam! I distinctly saw him just before he fell. He was reaching for the glider, but not touching it!" answered Phil.

All the men knew that they could trust Phil's judgment. He was a navy seal, after all. Once a seal, always a seal. Phil was sharp yet — at least sharper than Simon and maybe even sharper than Sam.

"Listen, boys," said Phil. "Whatever was going on here, you've got to come back to our cabin with us. We'll fix up that arm of yours and get you back in shape in no time. What are your names, by the way?"

"I'm Orville Right," said Orville.

"And I'm Wilbur," answered Orville's inventive friend.

"You've got to be kidding!" said Sam.

"About what?" said Orville.

"You both have the same first names as the Wright Brothers!" said Simon. "That's pretty weird!"

"Yeah, I suppose it is," said Wilbur. "Who were they, anyway?"

"Just the greatest inventors besides Henry Ford!" shouted Phil. "They invented the first airplane! Don't they teach you kids anything in school?"

"Well, we haven't been in school for quite a while," replied Orville. "It's a long story..." he said as he walked slowly down the trail toward the cabin. "Can I tell you more after I get some rest?"

"Sure, Orville!" said Sam. "You've had quite a day. Let's talk some more later. By the way, my name is Sam, and this is Simon here – the one who shot you two down."

"Gee thanks," answered Orville. "Nice to meet you... I think!"

With that said, Orville and Wilbur dragged their weary and worn bodies into the bunks of the old men's bedroom. They quickly fell asleep after having their wounds cared for, and the old men sat and wondered what they were going to do about these strange boys who had fallen from the sky and were now sleeping in their humble little dwelling.

9

When Orville and Wilbur woke up the next morning, they were pretty sore from their injuries and from landing in the trees the way they did. Orville's arm ached pretty badly from the few pieces of buckshot that had nicked him, and he noticed that one of the men had put a bandage on it while he was asleep. He was so worn out that he didn't even notice.

The two boys heard the old men snoring in the other room. They had given up their beds and found slumber in the arms of several Lazy-boys and an old dilapidated sofa. Simon's cheeks flapped back and forth with every snore, and Sam's handlebar mustache fluttered like a feather duster. Phil had never removed his hunting hat, and he was still out like a light too.

"Hey Orville!" whispered Wilbur. "What's that under the rug in the other room?"

"What? That seam there? Lift up the rug and check it out."

As Wilbur lifted up a flap of the rug, he noticed that there was a door of some kind built into the floor. He lifted it up and saw a secret stairway that led down below the home. The two fly-boys flicked a light switch on as they descended into the realm of the unknown. Who knew what they would find?

"Hey! Look!" said Orville. "All these pictures! That looks like Simon, standing next to that F-16 fighter jet! Whoa!

He was a pilot! And there's one of Sam too. I wonder if both of these guys were fighter pilots?"

"That's hard to believe!" replied Wilbur in shock. "Look at all these awards! These guys won medals! And look at all the kills on their planes! And there's one of Phil too. He's got a wetsuit on and an underwater spear. He must have been some kind of James Bond or something!"

Suddenly the boys heard footsteps on the floor above, and before they knew it, there were Sam, Simon, and Phil glaring at them through the trap-door. The three men walked down the stairs. The two fly-boys thought they were really in for it now. They didn't know what these military guys were like – whether they were friends or foes yet.

10

"So now you know the truth about us, don't you?" said Phil. "I guess we'll have to do something about that."

"What shall we do, boys?" asked Simon. "This is top-secret information. If news about us gets out, we could have some major trouble here. Spies from all over the world will be looking for us. This is bad all right...real bad."

"I guess we'll just have to take these boys for a one-way ride, huh?" said Sam.

Orville and Wilbur thought this was it. Their miserable short lives were about to be over. Sam and Simon had a little gleam in their eyes.

"Just kidding, guys! We didn't mean it!" laughed all three men.

"We're not spies or anything. We just did our time flying jets and fighting for Uncle Sam. That's all over now. But we do like flying - especially Sam and me!" said Simon.

"Well then, let me tell you the whole story!" said a relieved Orville. Orville went on to tell his whole life story, as well as his great escape. Simon and Sam believed him, but Orville had to actually fly over the cabin before Phil would believe it. Wilbur told his story too, and he was very sure to remember the part about Orville saving his life at the lighthouse.

"Wow, you boys are something else!" said Simon,

watching the flight over the cabin. "Why don't you come over to this barn over here. I've got something I think you might be interested in."

As the fearsome fivesome entered the barn, Orville and Wilbur saw something they had never experienced before. There, in full size, was an exact replica of one of the original Wright Brothers' early gliders. Though still under construction, she was a real beauty!

"How would you like to help us finish her off?" asked Sam. "I've seen what you guys can do. That little hang-glider you made was doing just fine until Si here showed up."

"Deal!" said the boys in unison. It was like they had one mind that thought the same thing at the same time.

It wasn't long before the men had to tell the authorities about the boys living with them. After hearing their stories during a lengthy legal process, the courts finally allowed the boys to live with Simon, Sam, and Phil. They really had no one else that cared about them. Over time, the five of them got along great. They tried to live as peacefully and privately as they could, and Orville and Wilbur went to school just like other boys their age. But they also spent many hours flying the ancient Wright brothers' machine over the vineyards and valleys of California. Everyone that saw the craft was entertained, especially when Orville was flying next to it and Wilbur was hang-gliding higher still above it. It was a sight to behold all right - a sight to behold! Even Orville and Wilbur Wright would have had a hard time believing it!

Made in the USA